Melodies of Hearts

Y Rohan

Ukiyoto Publishing

All global publishing rights are held by

Ukiyoto Publishing

Published in 2023

Content Copyright © Y Rohan

ISBN 9789359206424

*All rights reserved.
No part of this publication may be reproduced, transmitted, or stored in a retrieval system, in any form by any means, electronic, mechanical, photocopying, recording or otherwise, without the prior permission of the publisher.*

The moral rights of the authors have been asserted.

This is a work of fiction. Names, characters, businesses, places, events, locales, and incidents are either the products of the author's imagination or used in a fictitious manner. Any resemblance to actual persons, living or dead, or actual events is purely coincidental.

This book is sold subject to the condition that it shall not by way of trade or otherwise, be lent, resold, hired out or otherwise circulated, without the publisher's prior consent, in any form of binding or cover other than that in which it is published.

www.ukiyoto.com

Chords of Discovery

After going through endless classes and boring lectures, Alex came to the Music room. Not a soul was in sight and he sat before a piano in the middle of the room. The cupboards were neatly arranged with flutes and clarinets, and the drums and guitars were waiting to be played by people like him.

Alex looked outside through the window, the sky was orange, and the birds were returning home after a long day of hunting. He again turned his gaze towards the piano and started playing it. The sound echoed through the empty corridor.

As he finally ended his piece, someone from behind clapped for him, he turned around, and to his surprise, it was Olivia, the Student Council President. She smiled and slowly walked up to him.

"That was impressive, are you from the Music club?" she asked with a gentle tone.

"No. Those kids are not into classical music. I spend my time here with Mrs Daisy's permission," Alex replied while adjusting his glasses.

"Can you play that again for me?" she requested and took a seat before him.

Without saying a word, he again started playing. His hands moved like butter on the piano, and he was completely immersed in his art with his eyes closed. After playing for a few minutes, the piece ended.

"You are good. I play the violin, it's been a while though," Olivia said, standing up.

"I have written a piece, want to play with me?" Alex asked.

"Sure, but I'm not confident. How about tomorrow?" she suggested.

"Tomorrow's Sunday."

"How about Monday then?"

"I have a piano at home. Had to beg my Dad to buy me one. Eventually, he brought me a second-hand piano, it's not bad."

***

NEXT DAY

Around 10 AM, someone knocked on the door, Alex's Mom, Mitchelle, opened the door and was surprised to see Olivia.

"Hello, Mrs Michelle, I'm Alex's friend, Olivia," she said with a smile.

"Alex's friend?" Michelle said, surprised. "Come in."

A few minutes later, Alex came downstairs from his room after his Mom called him. Both of them sat in the adjoining room, where the piano was kept near the window.

"Wow, that's beautiful," Olivia said looking at the piano.

"Let's play," Alex said handing her paper with the musical score.

While they were playing, Alex's parents peeked from the hall, surprised to see their son with another human. Alex was never good at making friends, either he had been busy studying or playing the piano since childhood.

"My prayers are finally answered," Michelle said, wiping her tears of happiness.

"Come in, if you want to listen," Alex said looking at his parents. "By the way, I can hear you guys."

After an hour of playing and talking about music, the aromas of freshly prepared food filled the room. Both of them returned to the hall and Michelle told them to sit for lunch which Olivia politely declined.

"My son brings a friend home for the first time, this calls for a celebration. You will have to eat if you want to go home," Michelle said with a smile.

***

NEXT DAY

After classes had concluded, Alex sat all alone in his classroom, his gaze fixed on the children playing in the playground. Just then, Olivia arrived and her expression revealed surprise upon finding him in the classroom rather than the Music room, a place he often referred to as his paradise.

"What's wrong?" she asked taking a seat before him.

"Mrs Grace has told me to compose a piece and perform before school," he replied in a low voice while still looking outside.

"Isn't that something to be happy about?"

"Yes. For someone like you, yes, it is. But I have stage fright," Alex said, turning his gaze towards her.

"How about I help you then?" she suggested. "I regularly have to give speeches at school events, I can give you some tips.

There was a brief moment of silence, the noises of students could be heard from the playground and the chippering of birds from the nearby trees.

"Well, I don't want to fail Mrs Grace either, let's give it a try," Alex said with renewed confidence.

Both of them came to the Music room and as usual, it was empty except for Mrs Grace. She was reading a novel titled "A Song for Us." Mrs Grace looked at them, corrected her specs and smiled.

"Alex, it's nice to see you. Are you here to practice?" she asked.

"Yes, Mam," he replied politely while hiding his nervousness.

"And, what brings you here, Olivia?"

"I'm helping Alex to compose a musical score."

"In that case, I have something for you kids," saying that, she opened the cupboard and took out a paper with a song written on it and handed it to Alex.

"Is this to inspire me or something?" Alex asked, going through the paper.

"I found it in a dusty songbook in the old Music room. Supposedly, it was written by a pair of star-crossed lovers in the past, and now I want both of you to take inspiration from this and compose your very own piece for the performance."

"Me too?" Olivia asked surprised by the sudden offer to perform.

"You always loved to play the violin, but never got a chance due to your busy schedule. This is your chance to prove yourself," Mrs Grace replied walking around the room. "Next month I'm finally retiring, before I go, I want to see you both perform, the only kids who showed any interest in classical music."

"I won't let you down, Mam," Alex assured her.

"That's the spirit," she replied with a smile.

***

That evening when Alex returned home, he saw a few extra footwear outside his home. He sighed knowing that some strangers were inside and it was not going to be an easy evening. Once he entered, it was his aunt Rachel and her family. His Mom told him to get fresh up and join them for dinner.

Half an hour later, Alex comes downstairs and they sit around the table as his Mon starts serving the food. The first few minutes everything seemed to be alright, but nothing is permanent.

"Do you still sleep with a doll?" asked 16-year-old Ethan.

"I do. Still have that little boy with me," Alex replied and took a bite from his food.

Ethan tried his best to hold his laugh while his Mom glared at him in utter silence.

"You better apologize for what you said, Ethan," John, his dad said.

"Oh, I'm not offended, sir. When he used to pray to the tooth fairy to turn his broken teeth from the playground into gold coins, I was already well-versed in trigonometry," Alex said and calmly ate his food while everyone looked at him, speechless.

"Alex, apologize, now!" Mitchell said glaring at him.

"He started it. Tell him to apologize first," Alex replied.

"It's fine. They are kids," Rachel said, trying to de-escalate things.

***

FEW DAYS LATER

"I can't come up with anything," Alex said pacing up and down the Music room.

"We have a month left, relax. I'm going out with my friends, how about you join me?" Olivia suggested.

"How is that going to benefit me in any way?"

"Sometimes taking a walk in the park and coming back to work with a fresh mind helps a lot, trust me."

"Sounds like a plan," he said after a brief moment of thinking.

Nearly half an hour later, Olivia's friends, Mia and Ava arrived. The three girls giggled among themselves and had a small talk before they made their way out.

***

They came to the karaoke to scream out all the bottled-up emotions from the morning. Now Alex is not the type of guy who shows his emotions before people, not even to people who are close to him. So, obviously, this is a completely new experience for him.

Mia and Ava grabbed the mics and started singing, bringing out their inner singer. The songs were weird and their dances nearly scared the hell out of him.

"Are they your friends?" Alex whispered to Olivia in disbelief. "I thought someone like you chooses friends carefully."

"It's good to let go of yourselves once in a while," she whispered back.

After singing for some time and exhausting themselves, they collapsed on the long sofa. Olivia grabbed the mic to sing and her melodious voice grabbed Alex's complete attention and he listened to her with his full concentration.

"That was good," Alex said after she finished.

"Thanks," she replied sitting beside him.

"Won't you sing, pretty boy?" Mia asked.

"I can't," he replied in a low voice.

"He is shy, we are working on improving that," Olivia said.

Next, they came to a nearby café which is popular among teenagers. As expected, the café was fully packed, but they managed to find an empty table at the back and quickly sat around.

"Well, seniors, I appreciate that you all have accepted me tonight. This is the first time I have been out with kids around my age, something I thought I would never experience," Alex said as they waited for their food.

"I'm not trying to be rude, but why don't you have friends, Alex?" Olivia asked.

"Probably because I don't try to initiate a conversation with anyone, I guess," he replied. "Been like this since elementary school."

"That must have been rough," Mia said.

"I'm used to being alone. It has never been a problem to me, but my parents are concerned."

"Welcome to our group then," Ava said and smiled.

***

After a loud karaoke session, some snacks and sodas, they came out. The three girls giggled among themselves and waved goodbyes before they parted ways. Olivia and Alex walked side by side on the pathway. The cars and busses passed by them, and it soon started thundering followed by rain. They ran and took shelter under an empty bus stand.

"You said you haven't played the violin for quite some time... Can I know the reason?" Alex asked in a low voice as they waited for the rain to stop.

She looked at him, surprised. She clenched the left stripe of her bag tightly and smiled. "That came out of nowhere."

Sensing her hesitation, Alex tried to change the topic. "You don't have to tell me if you don't want to."

She sighed and looked at the sky. "It happened when I was in sixth grade. I had to perform before the entire school for an event. A day before that, I caught fever and collapsed because of the rigorous practice. I was scolded by my music teacher, relatives and a few other people... They said it was such a nice opportunity for me to showcase my skills as a violinist, and I ruined it."

"Th-that's tragic. When you can't give the results after you have been working hard for days, even months, sometimes," he said in a low voice.

"Right? Even I couldn't forgive myself. Even while all these things were happening, my parents never scolded me. They cheered for me to do better next time. After that, I didn't touch the violin till my first year of high school."

"Sorry to know that."

"When I saw you play the piano, it reignited my passion for playing the violin. Thanks," she said and smiled at him, and he smiled back.

***

"I'm home," Alex said opening the door.

"Wow, it's 8 PM, where have you been?" Michelle, his Mom asked.

"I went to karaoke with Olivia and her friends. Sounds unbelievable, I'm trying to comprehend too."

"Good. Get freshened up and we will have dinner," Michelle said walking towards the kitchen.

"Wait, aren't you gonna scold me for coming late?" he asked, a little surprised.

"It's fine. You made some friends. I have been waiting for a day like this for years."

Alex returned to the dining room after half an hour. The three of them sat around and his Mom started serving the food.

"The miracle has finally happened, huh?" his Dad said taking a bite from his food.

"You must be the first parents who are happy that their child is spending time out at night," he replied looking at them.

"Olivia seems to be a sweet girl. Till you are not hanging out with bad guys, everything's fine," Michelle said.

"I don't know how many parents say this, but... you don't have to always be attached with a book or play that piano all the time, social interactions and making friends is an important thing too, Alex," George said.

"You said something sensible after years," Michelle replied looking at him.

"If I don't study then how am I supposed to be number one in class? Your idea is rejected," Alex replied.

"I can't believe that someone like me has a son with an IQ of 150," George said.

"Well, it must have come from me."

"You finally said something funny after years," George said and laughed.

"You are sleeping on the couch today," Michelle said giving him a death stare.

"No!"

***

After nearly three weeks, and a lot of trial and error, Alex and Olivia finally managed to compose a piece, but Alex was still restless. Sensing his nervousness, Olivia grabbed his shoulder.

"Are you thinking about the performance?" she asked.

"Yes," he replied in a low voice. "Never tried something like this. Besides, what if I do something wrong? I won't be able to forgive myself."

"Self-doubt is normal for anyone, Alex. You will regret it for a lifetime if you don't perform at the cultural festival," she tried to make him understand.

"Y-you are right," he said looking at her with a smile.

"I have an idea, why don't we perform before the Music club members? It would help you with your stage fright," she suggested to which Alex agreed as he had no other option

***

The Music club has 20 members in total. You can hear their singing and music from far down the hallway. They often get told to lower their volumes or take their madness somewhere else.

The moment both of them entered the Club room, they spotted two club members Zoe and Andrew arguing among themselves near the stage.

"And your ideas are too relaxed, like a reggae rhythm. We need urgency and action, not just laid-back vibes," Zoe said.

"Your perspective is stuck in the past, like a classical composition. It's time to embrace modern methods," Andrew replied, folding his hands.

"Your plans are like a catchy pop song, repetitive and lacking depth. We need substance, not just a surface-level tune," she said glaring at him.

"And your ideas are too aggressive, like a pounding rock beat. We don't need to hit everything with brute force," he replied folding his hands and pulling faces to make her angrier.

"I think now you understand why I don't come here," Alex whispered.

"People settle down, we have the Student Council president here. Where are your manners?" said Alice the club leader. "What brings you here, Olivia?"

"We are making efforts to help Alex overcome his stage fright. I want all of you to listen to us play," Olivia requested.

All of them without saying a word took their seats before the stage and Alice gave a sign to both of them to get on the stage. There was an old piano covered with a dusty cloth, Alex gently sat before it looking at the crowd.

He took a deep breath and his hands started trembling. He tried to play but he couldn't bring himself to do it.

"If you are anxious, don't look at the crowd, close your eyes or look at the ceiling, this should be easy," Olivia encouraged who stood beside him with her violin.

"I have a solution," Alice said standing up. "Look at the person you are comfortable with. The person you spent a lot of time, it makes you calm."

But given Alex's past, he doesn't have any friends, and it didn't take them long to realize it.

Andrew raised his left eyebrow and folded his hands. "Do you play piano by ear? Because it sure sounds like your fingers aren't following any sheet music!" he said and laughed trying to make Alex feel relaxed.

"They say playing the piano relieves stress, but I have never seen anyone look more stressed while playing," Zoe joined him in the teasing.

"Look at them, Alex. They are here to encourage you, it's now or never," Olivia said looking at him.

***

FEW DAYS LATER

Alex is called to the school library after class hours by Olivia and her two friends. Expecting another outing with three beautiful girls, he makes his way to the library in quite a happy mood.

"So, seniors, why have I been summoned today?" Alex asked taking a seat facing Mia and Ava at the extreme end bench while Olivia sat beside him.

Mia started fidgeting and lowered her head a little. Alex sensed something was wrong but kept his silence as he didn't want to rush them into telling him, making them uncomfortable in the process.

"Come on, what are you waiting for? He's finally here," Ava said, frustrated.

"Wait, it's not that easy," Mia replied in a low voice, her face turned red and she seemed to be shy.

"We don't have all day. Alex has better things to do than this," Ava said, getting impatient.

"Ok, ok, calm down, honey badger," saying that Mia turned her gaze towards Alex and took a deep breath. "There's a guy named Lucas who I'm about to meet in a few days. I want to make a good impression... so, I want your opinions on a few stuffs."

"It lacks critical analysis. Think about it, senior. If you ask ten people to define happiness, all of them would have different answers. The same goes for dating preferences. Just because I'm a guy doesn't mean I can speak on behalf of every man on this planet," Alex replied.

"That's logical," Olivia agreed.

"So, what should I do?" Mia said trying to maintain her calm.

"You said he is from our school, right? Give me two days," saying that Alex stood up to leave.

***

TWO DAYS LATER

The four of them gathered in a nearby school cafeteria. The girls were excited to listen to what Alex had to say.

"A person's interests says a lot about them," Alex said looking at Mia who sat facing him. "I checked the school's library record book. Apparently, Lucas is into

'Love Unveiled' trilogy and two novels named 'Hearts Intertwined' and 'Forever Together.' What do you think?"

The three of them looked confused as their drinks arrived. Alex took a sip from his mango juice and sat back comfortably.

"What do you mean, Alex?" Mia asked swirling her drink.

"All of the novels I have mentioned have petite, sweet and fiercely intelligent women as the female lead, and they are also in leadership positions and can cook. So, if I'm not wrong, he's into women of that kind, senior," Alex explained.

"There's a flaw in your statement, Alex. What about people who admire charming villains or bad characters who just look good?" Olivia raised a question.

"That's a valid statement, senior. There are movies on villains way more famous than their nice counterpart, or their action figures getting oversold. That's because people only admire their outer beauty or their quirky behaviour, not their actions or personality," Alex replied. "Teenagers fall in love based on outer beauty, personality and behaviour is barely taken into consideration. And, that is also the reason why almost all relationships break up after a few months."

"What if he has a girlfriend?" Mia asked.

"I don't think he is dating anyone from our school," Alex replied.

"What about long-distance relationship? That's a possibility," Olivia asked.

"Everyone is at school till the club activities end, in other words till 5 PM. Since Lucas is a baseball player, he goes to a nearby academy after club activities. If I'm not wrong, the practice ends at 8 PM. Judging by his academic report, he's not bad, so he maybe studying after a long day," Alex replied.

"But that still doesn't prove your point, Alex," Ava said after finishing her drink.

"Think about it senior. Teenagers need a level of emotional maturity to sustain a long-distance relationship. We are still developing identities and gaining life experiences," Alex replied. "Even adults find it hard to keep up a long-distance relationship."

"You did a very good job of stalking him," Ava said.

"I didn't stalk him. I simply used the information available to me and came to a conclusion."

"Gosh, my mind is a mess," Mia said pulling her hair. "What should I do?"

"Hmm, the easiest way to get closer to someone is to share interests or act like your date's interests. On your first meeting, wear something casual but not overly casual. Stay away from dull colours but don't wear something too bright or dark either. You can act shy and clumsy, don't overdo it though. You should be fine if you follow these, but I can't tell if it would be 100 percent effective," Alex replied folding his hands.

"You are amazing, Alex," Olivia said.

"Thanks," he replied.

***

THE PERFORMANCE

The day finally arrived when Alex and Olivia would perform before the entire school during the cultural festival. Alex was overwhelmed by the crowd, it was not twenty people he performed for the past week, but a horde of people who would be staring at him in utter silence while he plays.

"We are finally doing this, huh?" Alex said taking a deep breath.

"We practised day and night for this moment, let's give it our all," Olivia replied, trying to motivate him.

"Well, thanks, senior. It would have been impossible without you."

"It is me who is lucky to perform beside a musical prodigy," she said and smiled.

Finally, the event started and they were called on to the stage to perform. Everyone looked at them eagerly, and this made Alex even more nervous. He looked around in the auditorium to find any familiar faces to keep his gaze upon and saw Mrs Grace in the front seat smiling at him, he smiled back and sat before his piano.

They started playing and everyone listened to them with their full attention. Alex looked at Mrs Grace and then closed his eyes, he did that a couple of times till he gained some confidence. He then tried looking at others, even though it was a little hard at first, he managed to do it after a few tries.

The performance ended and everyone stood up and clapped for them. Alex and Olivia looked at each other and smiled, acknowledging each other's contribution to this performance. One thing they knew, without each other's help, this would have been impossible. And now, they have done something they thought was impossible.

***

After a successful performance, Olivia suggested they go to an amusement park after her Dad gave her two tickets. At first, Alex was hesitant. He doesn't think risking one's life can be called amusement. After his parents kept on insisting, he had no other option than to join her.

"That's not amusing," Alex said looking at the deadly roller coaster. "What people define as amusing can be simply scary sometimes."

"Come on, it will be fun," saying that Olivia grabbed his hand and he silently sat beside her at the extreme back. The believer of science closed his eyes and prayed to God to spare his life.

The ride finally started and in a matter of seconds, they were up in the sky. The roller coaster slowed down providing a beautiful scenery of the entire amusement park, but that was short lived, the ride made its way down even faster as the tracks made a crackling sound.

As for Alex, his high-pitched voice stood out among his ride mates. Olivia grabbed his hand to calm him down.

Once the ride was over, they came out. For a moment, Alex sat on a bench like a statue trying to comprehend what just happened.

"A-are you alright? I should not have dragged you along with me," Olivia said looking at him, concerned.

"No. No, that was good. It's just that... I'm not used to stuff like this, senior. Not putting my life in danger to be precise."

"Let's try something of your choice then."

Next, they came to a Maze in a peaceful corner. It had relatively fewer people, most of them stuck in the maze. Their screams were clearly audible from the outside. Alex spotted a guy who finally made his way out, he jumped in joy and then kissed the ground as if he hadn't seen daylight in years.

There was a big map at the entrance of the maze for people to memorize, the only rule is not to write it anywhere. Alex looked at it for thirty seconds and then turned his gaze towards Olivia.

"Let's get in, senior."

"Wait, you memorized it already?" she asked, surprised.

"Yeah, I guess. Let's go."

They entered in. After walking for a few minutes, they spotted people simply wandering around, confused. Some started stomping on the ground while others pulled their hair. Alex calmly walked passed them. Seeing him all confident, some people who were stuck for quite some time started following him, and in fifteen minutes, they were finally out.

"See, I told you," Alex said looking at Olivia.

All the people who were saved by him started hugging him, few senior citizens kissed him on the forehead while able-bodied people lifted him. Before going everyone shouted their curses for the maze and went away.

"H-how?" Oliva asked, amazed, as they made their way towards other rides.

"Normally, people would try to memorize the map and use the words R, L, S. R for right, L for left and S for straight. But the thing is, people tend to get confused and jumble up the letters. As for me, I used Caesar code. First I memorized the map and turned the alphabets into code. H for R, N for L and O for S. It's easy for me to remember stuff that way when I don't have enough time."

"When you turn it into a code, it makes a meaningful word for you to remember, right?" she said.

"Yes. If we turn it into Caesar code, it would turn into. HO-NO-L-H-H."

"Hmm, I see. HO, NO and LHH. The first two words make sense and the last one can be easily memorized. You are amazing, Alex."

"Thanks," he said and smiled.

Next, they got on a swinging ship ride. The riders screamed in excitement as the ride gained momentum. This time, Olivia held his hand from the beginning, and Alex wasn't scared, and his full concentration was on the hand-holding thing.

The feeling of weightlessness tingled his stomach, but he kept his gaze on the hands.

***

They stopped by a monster-themed restaurant to have lunch. Even though the atmosphere was calm the room was all spooky.

"Here's your 'Death fried chicken with Dark sauce' and 'Hell's burger' Please enjoy," said the waiter with the sweetest voice in a dark suit as if he's just coming from a murder site after a successful killing spree.

"Let's go to the haunted house next. What do you say?" Olivia suggested.

"Even though I don't believe in monsters or ghosts, they sure are creepy, senior," he replied before taking a bite from his burger.

"Is that a yes?"

***

To end the day, they got on the Ferris wheel. The brightly lit amusement Park was clearly visible from this height. They took some pictures together and enjoyed the view.

Olivia scrolled through her phone and showed the photos to Alex which she took from the morning.

"Whoa, I look ugly," he said.

"You were scared for sure," she replied, giggling.

"I had fun, senior. I have never been to an amusement park except with my parents," he said and smiled.

"Well, it's time that you start making friends," she replied.

"I will give it a try then."

THE END

About the Author

Y Rohan is the author of My Chaos Life. He has also self-published two of his novels. He graduated high-school from Kendriya Vidyalaya Sanghatan, and is currently studying in college. He spends his leisure time either reading or working on his novels. He unconditionally loves dark fantasy and science fiction genre. He believes hard work and dedication can open doors for newer opportunities and success.

www.ingramcontent.com/pod-product-compliance
Lightning Source LLC
LaVergne TN
LVHW041643070526
838199LV00053B/3537